THE AMERICAN GIRLS

1764 KAYA, an adventurous Nez Perce girl whose deep love for horses and respect for nature nourish her spirit

1774 FELICITY, a spunky, spritely colonial girl, full of energy and independence

1824  JOSEFINA, an Hispanic girl whose heart and hopes are as big as the New Mexico sky

1854  KIRSTEN, a pioneer girl of strength and spirit who settles on the frontier

1864  ADDY, a courageous girl determined to be free in the midst of the Civil War

1904 SAMANTHA, a bright Victorian beauty, an orphan raised by her wealthy grandmother

1934 KIT, a clever, resourceful girl facing the Great Depression with spirit and determination

1944 MOLLY, who schemes and dreams on the home front during World War Two

1904

MEET
Samantha
An American Girl

BY SUSAN S. ADLER
ILLUSTRATIONS DAN ANDREASEN
VIGNETTES RENÉE GRAEF

American Girl

Visit our Web site at **americangirl.com**

Printed in China.
05 06 07 08 09 10 LEO 66 65 64 63 62 61

The American Girls Collection®, Samantha Parkington®, Samantha™,
and American Girl® are trademarks of American Girl, LLC.

PICTURE CREDITS
The following individuals and organizations have generously given
permission to reprint illustrations contained in "Looking Back": p. 55—Museum
of the City of New York, Byron Collection; pp. 56–57—Museum of the City of New York,
Byron Collection; New York State Historical Association, Cooperstown; Charles Ranhofer,
The Epicurean (Dover Publications, Inc., New York, 1971); pp. 58–59—Jim Harter,
Food and Drink (Dover Publications, Inc., New York, 1980);
Wisconsin Historical Society, Charles Van Schaick and
McCormick Collections; pp. 60–61—Museum of the City of New York,
Byron Collection; Photographic Archives, Special Collections, University
of Kentucky Libraries; Culver Pictures.

Cover Background by Paul Bachem

Library of Congress Cataloging-in-Publication Data

Adler, Susan, S. 1946–
Meet Samantha : an American girl / by Susan S. Adler ;
illustrations, Dan Andreasen ; vignettes, Reneé Graef.
p. cm. — (The American girls collection)
Summary: In 1904, nine-year-old Samantha, an orphan living
with her wealthy grandmother, and her servant friend Nellie have a
midnight adventure when they try to find out what has happened
to the seamstress who suddenly left her job.
ISBN 0-937295-80-9 (hardcover) — ISBN 0-937295-04-3 (pbk.)
[1. Friendship—Fiction. 2. Household employees—Fiction.
3. Women—Suffrage–Fiction.]
I. Andreasen, Dan, ill. II. Title. III. Series.
PZ7.A26155 Me 1998   [Fic] — dc21   98-16815   CIP   AC

TO MY PARENTS,
WHO MADE CHILDHOOD
BEAUTIFUL

TABLE OF CONTENTS

SAMANTHA'S FAMILY
AND FRIENDS

CHAPTER ONE
JESSIE   1

CHAPTER TWO
A NEW GIRL   11

CHAPTER THREE
THE TUNNEL   21

CHAPTER FOUR
GONE!   28

CHAPTER FIVE
NIGHT VISIT   35

CHAPTER SIX
A FINE YOUNG LADY   47

LOOKING BACK   55

SNEAK PEEK   63

SAMANTHA'S FAMILY

GRANDMARY
*Samantha's
grandmother, who
wants her to be a
young lady*

NELLIE
*The girl who
lives—and works—
next door*

SAMANTHA
*A nine-year-old
orphan who lives
with her wealthy
grandmother*

UNCLE GARD
*Samantha's
favorite uncle, who
calls her "Sam"*

CORNELIA
*An old-fashioned
beauty who has
newfangled ideas*

HAWKINS
*Grandmary's butler
and driver, who is
Samantha's friend*

MRS. HAWKINS
*The cook, who
always has a treat
for Samantha*

JESSIE
*Grandmary's
seamstress, who
"patches
Samantha up"*

ELSA
*The maid, who
is usually grumpy*

EDDIE
*Samantha's
neighbor, who loves
to tease*

JESSIE

"Samantha!"

The voice broke through the summer afternoon like a crack. The leaves of the quiet old oak tree suddenly rustled and dropped a squirming bundle of arms and legs. Samantha Parkington tumbled out of the tree.

"Samantha, you're really dumb," the voice continued. It was coming from a hole in the hedge that separated Samantha's house from Eddie Ryland's. "You're so dumb, you don't even know how to climb a tree."

Samantha glanced at her scraped and bleeding knee and looked pained—not because of the knee, but because the voice was at it again. She glared at

1

its owner with a look that could have frozen water in July. "Go away, Eddie."

But Eddie's round, sticky face didn't go away. "You're so dumb, you probably think three times four is twelve," he said.

"Eddie." Samantha looked disgusted. "Three times four *is* twelve."

"Well, anyway, you're so dumb—"

That was enough for Samantha. "Eddie," she said, "if you don't get out of here right now, I will take your entire beetle collection from behind the shed, and I'll put it in the offering plate at church on Sunday." She paused to be sure he was listening. "And I'll tell your mother *you* did it."

Eddie's eyes grew wide. He pulled his mouth into a frog face and left to find a safer hiding place for his beetle collection.

Samantha examined her knee. The bleeding had stopped, but her stocking was badly torn. She could picture how Grandmary would look when she saw it. Grandmary's eyes had a soft, warm light when they looked at Samantha, but her face could be very stern when she talked about

2

growing up. "Discipline," Grandmary always said, "is what turns girls into ladies."

Samantha tugged at the hole in her stocking, but she couldn't hide it. The taffeta bow that had held her dark brown hair drooped over her forehead. Yes, this was a job for Jessie.

Samantha hurried up the walk and climbed the porch steps two at a time. At the front door, she slowed down. If there was any noise at the front door, Elsa might come. Elsa was the new maid. She was always grumpy, and Samantha didn't want to listen to a lecture now.

Luckily, the door was quiet. No one saw Samantha run all the way to the third floor. There, at the end of the hall, was the sewing room. And in the corner sat Jessie. Yards and yards of soft pink material tumbled around her, and the sewing machine clicked quietly as her feet pressed the treadle back and forth. She hummed to its rhythm as her fine hands guided the cloth past the flashing needle.

Jessie made clothes for the household. She was working on a new dress for Grandmary, but she stopped as Samantha came through the door.

"Oh, Miss Samantha, just look at you," Jessie said. As she stood and turned, Jessie's large floating apron swirled over the baskets of thread and laces that rested on the floor. "What have you been up to? No, don't tell me. I don't want to know. Here you are, nine years old, almost a lady, and still getting into mischief like a ragamuffin. What will your Grandmary say?"

Samantha folded her hands and looked at the floor until Jessie was quiet. The mild scolding was a small price to pay for the help she knew Jessie would give her. Already Jessie had brushed the

"Here you are, nine years old, almost a lady, and still getting into mischief like a ragamuffin," said Jessie.

grass and dust from her hair. Now she checked Samantha's dress for tears and stains. She spotted the torn stocking.

"Take off those shoes and stockings right now. Does your knee hurt?" asked Jessie.

"No, Jessie, it's all right. I'd just rather not have to explain to Grandmary," said Samantha.

Jessie smiled and reached for her sewing basket. Samantha found a small clean rag and wet it from the water pitcher. She sponged her injured knee while Jessie sat down to repair the damaged stocking.

As Samantha looked around the room, she noticed a piece of jelly biscuit on the floor. She must have dropped it the day before. Three ants had found it. She was about to tell Jessie when she noticed two more ants on their way. It would be fun to see how many would come.

Samantha sighed loudly. "It must be awfully boring to be grown up," she said.

Jessie laughed softly. "Well, that depends. It depends a lot on the person. Now you, Miss Samantha, I don't think you'll have to be worried about being bored, even when you're grown up."

There were seven ants on the jelly biscuit now.

"I'll bet Cornelia isn't bored," said Samantha. Jessie laughed again. "No, I don't imagine Miss Cornelia is very often bored," she said. Cornelia was a friend of Samantha's favorite uncle. She was pretty and dark haired, and she laughed easily. Anyone could see that she liked Uncle Gard a lot. But Samantha didn't think Cornelia was right for Uncle Gard. She thought someone like Alice Roosevelt, the President's daughter, would be better. Alice Roosevelt did the most exciting things, and the newspapers were always talking about her.

"Is Uncle Gard going to marry Cornelia?" asked Samantha.

Alice Roosevelt

"That's none of our business," Jessie said firmly. "And children shouldn't ask such questions."

Samantha grumbled softly. "A minute ago I was almost a lady. Now I'm a child again."

Twelve ants were on the biscuit, and three were on the way.

"Uncle Gard is a spy, you know," Samantha said.

"Miss Samantha!" Jessie's head shot up in surprise. "Where do you get such foolish ideas?"

"Well, he *should* be a spy," Samantha went on. "He's so handsome and brave, everyone would just fall in love with him. He could get their secrets, and they'd be so in love with him, they wouldn't even care."

"I think you'd better keep such ideas to yourself," Jessie said as she looked closely at the hole she was mending. "You've made quite enough trouble for one day."

There were nineteen ants around the jelly biscuit.

"Jessie, did you know my mother and father?" Samantha asked.

Jessie spoke gently. "You know I didn't, child. That accident in the boat happened when you were just five. You know I didn't come to work for your grandmother till you were seven."

Samantha had known that. Asking had really been wishing. She touched the locket pinned to her dress. Inside the small gold heart was a picture of her mother and father. She would have loved to hear Jessie talk about them. When Jessie told stories, she made everything sound like magic. Jessie would have made Samantha's parents seem like a prince and princess.

"Tell me about New Orleans, Jessie. Please?"

Jessie picked up a piece of silk for the sleeve of Grandmary's new dress. Her musical voice began to tell about a place where flowers bloomed in winter, a place where there were huge white mansions and balconies made of iron that looked like lace. She told about spicy shrimp and about music and dancing in the streets. And the best part was, everything Jessie said was true. She didn't have to make up stories about faraway places. Her husband, Lincoln, was a porter on the train that ran to New Orleans. Lincoln brought home wonderful tales of the places he'd seen and the people he'd met. And he never forgot Samantha. She had a scrapbook almost full of colorful postcards that he sent her from all of his trips. Sometimes he brought her pralines from New Orleans—brown sugary candy crowded with sweet pecans. Jessie and Lincoln made Samantha's world wide and wonderful. An hour passed easily with Jessie's soft voice carrying Samantha to dreamlike places.

CHAPTER
TWO
—

A NEW GIRL

At four o'clock, Samantha stood
outside the parlor doors, looking like
new. It was time for her hour with
Grandmary. Samantha's hair was combed, her
ribbon was perfect, her skirt hung straight, and her
stockings were repaired. She knocked softly on the
door, then slipped through and made a quick curtsy
to her grandmother.

Samantha thought Grandmary looked like
a queen, especially during their sewing hour.
Grandmary sat up very straight. Her velvet chair
looked like a throne with her silk gown flowing
around it. Her white hair seemed made for a crown,
with never a strand out of place.

Samantha always *tried* to be a young lady, but it was a lot easier to remember how when Grandmary was watching. Samantha noticed that everyone behaved more like a lady when Grandmary was around.

"Good afternoon, Samantha," said Grandmary.

"Good afternoon, Grandmary." Samantha squirmed ever so slightly. She didn't know how, but Grandmary always seemed to know when she had been into mischief. But today Grandmary didn't ask questions. Instead, she smiled.

"Come sit down, my dear," Grandmary said.

She handed a small basket to Samantha. "You must try to work a little harder on your sampler. It's not going very quickly."

"Yes, Grandmary." Samantha took her seat on a chair next to her grandmother. She picked up her sampler and sighed a little. When it was finished, the sampler would read "ACTIONS SPEAK LOUDER THAN WORDS." Grandmary had explained this saying. She said it meant that how people act is more important than what they say. Samantha tried to imagine the words sewn in pink silk thread. Around them would be flowers and fruits made of complicated stitches that would show off her sewing skills. But the skills were slow in coming. So far the sampler read "ACTIONS SP."

Samantha stuck her tongue between her lips as she concentrated on a hard stitch. She glanced sideways to see if her grandmother looked in a good mood.

"Grandmary," Samantha began.

"Yes, dear?"

"Did you see the doll in Schofield's shop?" Samantha asked.

"Yes, dear, I did," answered Grandmary.

"Isn't she beautiful?" sighed Samantha.

"It's quite a nice doll," Grandmary said.

"Do you think I might have her?"

"Samantha, that is an expensive doll," said Grandmary. "It costs six dollars. If you are going to grow up to be a responsible young lady, you must understand the value of a dollar."

"I could earn the money to buy her, Grandmary. I could make boomerangs and sell them. *The Boys' Handy Book* shows just how to do it. I could—"

"Samantha!" Grandmary was shocked. "A *lady* does not earn money."

Samantha had known there wasn't much hope, but she added very quietly, "Cornelia says a woman should be able to earn money. She says women shouldn't have to depend on men for everything. She says—"

"Cornelia has a great many newfangled

notions," announced Grandmary. "She should keep them to herself."

Samantha turned back to her work with a sigh. "I would have called the doll Lydia," she said softly. "She looks like my mother."

Grandmary was startled. Then her eyes softened. A moment later she said, "There are other ways, my dear, to reach your goals."

Samantha looked up hopefully. Grandmary continued, "If you do well at your tasks, you might earn the doll. If you practice your piano daily—"

"Oh, Grandmary, I will." Samantha was delighted. "I'll practice an hour every day. I'll make my sampler beautiful. I'll help Mrs. Hawkins. I won't get my dress muddy. I—" She was about to say she wouldn't tease Eddie Ryland, but she knew there were some promises she just couldn't keep. "Oh, Grandmary, thank you!" Samantha threw her arms around her grandmother's neck.

"There, there, my dear. We shall see," said Grandmary with a slight note of caution in her voice. "We shall see how you do."

Samantha worked hard on her sampler for half an hour. Then, from down the street, she heard a low

rumble. Soon there were great pops and bangs.
As the noise grew louder, angry voices and the
frightened whinnies of horses joined it. Samantha
jumped up from her seat and ran to the window.

"Oh, Grandmary, it's Uncle Gard. It's Uncle
Gard and Cornelia!" Samantha called.

Grandmary raised her eyes to the ceiling. "He's
brought that dreadful automobile again. Whatever
shall I tell the neighbors!"

Samantha could hardly contain her excitement
as the shiny black car jerked and sputtered to a stop
in front of the house. Two people climbed out. They
wore long coats that covered them from head to toe.
Cornelia wore a hat tied down with a scarf, and
Uncle Gard wore large goggles that made him look
like an overgrown fly. They came up the walk laughing and beating the dust from their hats and coats.

The bell rang. A minute later, Hawkins appeared
at the parlor door looking dignified. It seemed to
Samantha that the more confusion there was, the
more dignified Hawkins became. "Mister Gardner
and Miss Cornelia, Madam," he said.

"Very well, Hawkins. Show them in. And tell
Elsa to bring tea," said Grandmary.

"Oh, Grandmary, it's Uncle Gard.
It's Uncle Gard and Cornelia!" Samantha called.

The couple burst into the room, bringing laughter and the smell of summer with them. "How are you, Mother? You look wonderful," said Uncle Gard. He gave Grandmary a big hug, and she couldn't help smiling.

"Good afternoon, Gardner. Good afternoon, Cornelia," said Grandmary. "I am fine, thank you, Gardner. But I was a good deal better before you shattered the peace of the entire neighborhood with that horrible machine of yours. Why must you bring it here?"

Uncle Gard's eyes were laughing. "Now, Mother, this is 1904. You've got to keep up with the times. Besides," he winked at Samantha, "how can I teach Sam to drive if I don't bring the automobile?"

"Oh, Uncle Gard, will you really? Will you?" Samantha was popping with excitement.

"Sure I will. Come on. I'll take you for a ride right now."

"Indeed, you won't," said Grandmary. "What can you be thinking of? Why, her clothes would be ruined!"

Samantha's face fell.

Cornelia looked at her quickly and
said, "It's all right. She can wear my
duster. It's a little too big, but we'll
make it fit, won't we, Samantha?"

As they walked into the hall to
fix the coat, Samantha gave Cornelia

duster

a grateful smile. Minutes later, she headed down the
walk, trailing the hem of the long coat behind her.

Eddie Ryland had been sitting in the car, but he
scampered down as Samantha and her uncle
approached.

Uncle Gard lifted Samantha up to the seat.
"Hold tight, Sam, while I crank it up," he said.

"You sure look dumb, Samantha," Eddie teased.
He never stopped.

Samantha wasn't listening. She held tight as
Uncle Gard cranked and the car began to lurch.

"Anyway, I know something you don't know,"
Eddie said loudly so that Samantha could hear him
as the car rumbled.

Uncle Gard jumped into the seat next to
Samantha and took hold of the steering wheel. The
car began to bounce and sway into the middle of
the road.

"A girl's coming to live at our house. She's nine, just like you," Eddie hollered over the noise.

"You're lying, Eddie Ryland!" Samantha yelled and choked on the dust.

"I am not! Her name's Nellie!"

Samantha didn't even try to answer. She was holding on for dear life as that most modern of inventions, the automobile, bucked and rumbled its way toward town.

Back at the front door, Grandmary shook her head. Just as she turned back to the parlor to join Cornelia for a cup of tea, she saw Jessie scurrying from the kitchen. There was something in her hand.

"Jessie, what's the matter?" asked Grandmary.

As Jessie hurried up the stairs, she called over her shoulder, "It's pepper for the sewing room, ma'am. There are ants up there. Hundreds and hundreds of ants!"

THE TUNNEL

Several days later, Samantha bounded into her backyard holding a gingerbread cookie. She had just finished practicing the piano. She practiced piano every day now, for one whole hour. That hour certainly did seem long. She couldn't wait to get outside when it was over.

Samantha took a deep breath of summer air and a couple of long leaps. She stopped beside the tunnel.

The tunnel was a hole worn in the lilac hedge between her house and the Rylands', but Samantha had always called it "the tunnel." Through it now, she could see a girl. The girl was busy hanging laundry in the Rylands' yard. Could Eddie possibly have been telling the truth? Had this girl really come to live there? Samantha ducked through the tunnel and came closer.

"Are you Nellie?" she asked brightly.

The girl looked surprised and very timid. "Yes, miss," she answered without stopping her work. Eddie had said Nellie was nine, but this girl seemed smaller than Samantha.

"Are you visiting the Rylands?" asked Samantha.

This time Nellie looked amused. "Oh, no, miss. I'm working here," she said.

Samantha was surprised. Eddie hadn't said a girl was coming to *work*. But it didn't matter. Samantha thought it would be wonderful to have a friend right next door. She remembered the cookie in her hand. "Would you like some gingerbread?" she asked. "It's just baked."

Nellie looked at the Rylands' house. "Oh, no, miss. I can't."

"Won't they let you?" asked Samantha.

"No, I don't think so, miss. I've got my job to do," Nellie answered.

"My name's Samantha. You don't have to call

me 'miss.'" Samantha put her cookie and napkin down on a stone and reached for a piece of wet laundry. "I'll help you, Nellie. Then we can play."

"Oh, no, you shouldn't," Nellie said. She was embarrassed, but there was nothing she could do to stop her new friend. So instead, she hurried to finish the job before anyone could see Samantha working.

When the last of the laundry was hung, Samantha grabbed Nellie's hand and pulled her toward the tunnel. "We can eat in here. Nobody will see us," Samantha said. The girls just fit into the hole in the hedge, and Nellie couldn't say no to the spicy smell of gingerbread.

"Why are you working here?" Samantha asked between bites.

Nellie didn't look at Samantha when she answered. "My father works in a factory in the city, and my mother does washing. But there's three of us children, you see, and it's not enough." She added quietly, "There wasn't enough food. And there wasn't enough coal."

Samantha's eyes were wide with disbelief. She

was good at imagining castles and jungles and sailing ships, but she had never imagined hunger and cold. "You mean your parents sent you away? But that's awful!"

"Oh, no. It's better here. It really is," said Nellie. "The Rylands pay my family a dollar a week for the work I do. That's not as much as I earned in the factory, but in the factory I had to work every day but Sunday, until dark. And the air was so hot and dusty, I started coughing a lot. That's why my parents let me come here. The air is good, and I don't have to work so long, and I get good food." With one finger, she collected the last of the cookie crumbs. "Only I don't get to see my family much."

Samantha was shocked into silence, but only for a moment. "When do you go to school?" she asked.

"I've never been to school," Nellie said quietly.

Was it possible? This girl had never gone to school? Samantha's mind raced. "Nellie, I have an idea," she said. "We can meet here every day, and I'll teach you. The Rylands won't miss you for just a little while, and I'll teach you *everything*."

Nellie's eyes glittered with excitement as the

"There wasn't enough food. And there wasn't enough coal,"
said Nellie.

girls made plans. Then Samantha began talking about everyone she lived with and all the neighbors. By the time she'd told Nellie about Uncle Gard's automobile, they were both giggling.

The girls were interrupted by a familiar voice. "I see you, Samantha! I see you, Nellie! And you're really ugly. You're both so ugly, you'd scare a moose. You're so ugly—"

"Eddie, get out of here," Samantha snapped.

"I'm telling!"

Eddie started toward the house. Nellie looked frightened, but Samantha yelled "Eddie!" in a voice that made him think he'd better wait to hear what she had to say. "Eddie, if you tell anybody anything about us, I will take your new pocketknife and I will stuff it full of taffy."

Eddie stopped. He stared at Samantha. Then he put his hand over his back pocket to protect his knife. He began to back away from the girls. Finally, he ran away.

When he'd gone, Nellie jumped up. "I'd better get back to work," she said.

Samantha followed her out of the tunnel. "All right. But tomorrow we'll make a telephone.

Mrs. Hawkins will give us two tin cans, and I can get a string. We'll string it through the hedge, where Eddie won't see it. Then we can talk whenever we want to. Oh, Nellie, we'll have the most wonderful time!"

GONE!

By next Tuesday afternoon, Samantha's
sampler read "ACTIONS SPEAK LOUDER
THA." The sewing hour was almost over
when there was a gentle knock on the parlor door.

"Come in," said Grandmary, and Jessie came in
dressed to leave for home. She curtsied quickly and
waited for Grandmary to speak.

Samantha thought Jessie always looked elegant.
She was so tall and held her head so high. Jessie
looked especially grand today. She was wearing a
light brown summer coat that came almost to the
floor. But Samantha wondered why she was leaving
so early.

"Yes, Jessie?" questioned Grandmary.

"Ma'am, I've just come to say I won't be coming back now," Jessie said.

Samantha almost jumped out of her chair. "Jessie! Why?" she asked.

Grandmary silenced her with a look that said children should be seen and not heard. She spoke to Jessie. "Very well, Jessie. I'd like to thank you for your service. You have been a great help and a pleasure to us. We shall miss you very much."

Samantha was horrified. What was Grandmary saying? How could she just let Jessie go away like that?

"You can see Hawkins for your pay," continued Grandmary. "There will be a bonus for you."

Jessie curtsied again. "Thank you, ma'am." Before she left she stopped to smile at Samantha. "Be very good, Miss Samantha. You know I'll miss you."

Samantha was too stunned to answer. She watched Jessie go. Then her words rushed out. "Grandmary, why is Jessie leaving? And why did you let her?"

Grandmary's eyes never moved from the lace-work in her hands. "Please sit down, Samantha,"

*Samantha almost jumped out of her chair.
"Jessie! Why?"*

she said. "A young lady must not ask questions of her elders. This is Jessie's business."

Samantha sat down, but she could only fidget with her sewing. It seemed as if every stitch she put in her sampler had to be pulled out again. She didn't understand. Why would Jessie leave without explaining?

At last the sewing hour was over. Samantha curtsied quickly when Grandmary excused her. Then she rushed out of the parlor to find Mrs. Hawkins, the cook.

There was never any problem finding Mrs. Hawkins. She was always in the kitchen. And the kitchen was always filled with the wonderful smells of Mrs. Hawkins's cooking. Today she stood by the big wooden table in the center of the room, rolling pastry for meat pie. She wasn't surprised to see Samantha. The kitchen was one of Samantha's favorite places. She came there often to talk and to eat the treats Mrs. Hawkins saved for her.

"Hello, love," Mrs. Hawkins said. "Why are you rushing so? Sit down now and tell me what's the matter. You look like thunder."

Samantha flopped herself down on a chair. "Jessie's gone away," she said.

"Yes, dear, I know."

Mrs. Hawkins knew? Everybody knew but Samantha! She brushed away a fly that buzzed in from the open windows. "But why?" she asked. "Grandmary didn't even try to stop her!"

"Now, now, love. You must not fret about it," Mrs. Hawkins said. She took an onion from a bunch hanging by the door and began to peel it. "There are some things you just don't understand. Don't you think your Grandmary knows best?"

How could Samantha possibly know if Grandmary knew best? How could she know if anybody knew best? She didn't know what anybody knew!

She pushed back her chair and hurried from the kitchen to the butler's pantry. She hoped Hawkins would be there, and he was. Hawkins was whistling softly and polishing silver. He pulled out a chair for Samantha. He was used to her popping up in strange places. They had their best talks when Samantha followed him around on his jobs, waxing furniture, beating the carpets, or washing the windows in Grandmary's big house. Now Hawkins handed Samantha a polishing cloth. He knew how much easier it is to talk when your hands are busy.

Samantha rubbed at a sugar bowl. "Jessie's gone," she said.

"I know," said Hawkins. Samantha wasn't surprised.

"Nobody will tell me why," Samantha went on.

Hawkins smiled, and his eyes were understanding. But when he spoke, it didn't help much. "Believe me, Miss Samantha, Jessie's fine," he said. "I know it isn't easy, but sometimes, when you're young, you just have to trust."

Samantha didn't feel much like talking anymore. She pushed back the sugar bowl and cloth, straightened her chair, and slowly left the pantry. As she shuffled past the parlor, Grandmary called, "Samantha."

"Yes, ma'am?"

"I have been very pleased with your efforts these past weeks," Grandmary said. "If you go upstairs, you will find something on your bed."

For a minute Samantha forgot about Jessie's leaving. She even forgot to say thank you as she ran up the stairs two at a time. Inside her room, Samantha stopped short. There in the middle of her bed was a doll dressed in shining blue silk. She had a wide silk hat to match. Her soft china hands and face were rosy and delicate. "Oh, Lydia," Samantha whispered. She picked the doll up gently. Then she hugged her very close.

NIGHT VISIT

The next morning, Samantha brought Lydia to meet Nellie in the tunnel. But when she saw how Nellie's eyes glowed and how gently she touched Lydia's dress, Samantha wondered if she had been wrong to bring the doll. Nellie had never owned a doll, not even a simple doll, and certainly not a doll as beautiful as Lydia.

"It's all right if you play with her," Samantha said. "Look. Her hat can come off and her dress even has little buttons."

While Nellie cradled Lydia, Samantha told her what had happened.

"Jessie left, and nobody will tell me why," Samantha said.

Nellie didn't answer. She was buttoning the tiny buttons.

"I think I know, though," Samantha continued. "I think she's going to be an actress."

Nellie carefully removed Lydia's hat and turned it over in her hand.

"She'll be famous," Samantha went on. "And one day she'll come back here, and we'll go to see her. And she'll take you and me to meet all the actors and actresses. Only you and me, out of the whole town. Because we were her friends."

Nellie still had nothing to say. Now she was

looking at the doll's tiny leather shoes.

In the days that followed, Samantha came up with several reasons for Jessie's leaving. Maybe Jessie had gone to New Orleans with Lincoln, to be a singer there. Jessie had a beautiful voice. Or the President might have asked her to be a spy in Europe. She'd sew elegant clothes for kings and queens and learn their secrets. Or maybe her brother had been kidnapped and taken to South America, and Jessie was going to rescue him.

Then one day Nellie had a suggestion. "Maybe she's got a baby," Nellie said.

Samantha was startled. "Why would she do that?"

Nellie shrugged. "Lots of people do. They just like babies," she said.

Samantha had to agree. "Jessie loves babies."

"Well then?"

Samantha was annoyed. Nellie's idea wasn't half as exciting as any of hers. But it was too sensible to be ignored. "Why wouldn't Grandmary tell me if it was a baby?" asked Samantha.

Nellie shrugged again. "Grownups don't like to talk about babies coming."

Samantha had to agree. "I asked Grandmary about babies once, and she said it wasn't a proper subject for young girls."

Nellie nodded in understanding.

"I asked Mrs. Hawkins, and she said the stork brings babies. But she wouldn't talk about it anymore," Samantha continued.

"I don't think it's true anyway," said Nellie. "When my baby sister came, the midwife was at our building. My other sister and I had to go out with my uncle. When we got back, my baby sister was there and the midwife was fixing tea for my mother. But there wasn't any stork anywhere."

Samantha was puzzled. "What's a midwife?" she asked.

"She's a lady who visits whenever a new baby comes," Nellie answered. "My uncle said she brings the baby in her little black bag. But I looked in, and the bag was full of things like doctors have. There wouldn't be any room for a baby in there."

"Nellie, we've just *got* to find out what happened to Jessie," said Samantha. "If we just

knew where she lived, we could ask Lincoln.
He must know where she is."

"I know where she lives," said Nellie.

Samantha's eyes were wide with surprise.
"You do?"

Nellie nodded. "A woman across the street
from Jessie makes an herb tea that cures headaches.
One day Mrs. Ryland wanted some, so she sent me
home with Jessie to get it. I can show you."

Samantha hugged her. "Oh, Nellie, that's
perfect! Only we can't go in the daytime. They'd
stop us for sure. We'll go tonight. When everyone's
in bed, I'll sneak down the back stairs and meet
you right here in the tunnel. Look out your window
and watch my house. Grandmary always turns out
the gas lamps just before she goes to bed. That's
how you'll know it's all right for me to come down
and meet you."

Nellie agreed. She knew that no one at the
Ryland house would even notice if she went out
after she had finished her evening chores.

39

Samantha had always thought the nighttime was very quiet, but that night, noises seemed to come from everywhere. The crickets were making a terrible racket. The bushes and trees rustled as though they were hiding wild animals, and dogs barked all around. Samantha closed the back door carefully and hurried to the tunnel to find Nellie.

The two girls held hands and started out of the yard and up the street. As long as they were on familiar streets, where gas lamps glowed with a friendly light, they thought their adventure was grand and very exciting. But after they crossed the railroad tracks, the streets got dark and narrow. The houses were dark, too, and very small. Somewhere there was loud music and noisy laughter, and once in a while there was shouting. Nellie squeezed Samantha's hand so tightly that Samantha couldn't have let go if she'd wanted to. But she certainly didn't want to. She was just as frightened as her friend was. *Maybe we shouldn't have come at all,* she thought. But she didn't say that to Nellie. She wanted to be brave.

"Are you sure you know the way?" Samantha whispered.

"I—I think so." Nellie's voice was shaky. "It's not much farther now."

Samantha looked at the drab houses they were passing. Even in the dark she could tell there wasn't much grass in front, and there was very little room for flowers. "Why does Jessie live here?" she asked.

"This is the colored part of town," Nellie answered.

"You mean Jessie *has* to live here?" Samantha asked.

Nellie looked at her. Samantha was smart about so many things that Nellie was always surprised at what her friend didn't know. "Yes, of course," Nellie said.

"Why?" asked Samantha.

"I don't know," Nellie said. "It's just the way grownups do things." Her face lit up with relief. "There it is," she said. The soft glow of a kerosene lamp shone from a window, and the girls rushed to the wall beneath it. They huddled there for a minute, panting.

"Aren't you going to knock on the door?" Nellie whispered.

Samantha suddenly lost her nerve. "What if it's not the right house after all?" she said. "Or what if Jessie went away with Lincoln, and somebody else lives there now?"

"Well, we can look in the window," said Nellie. "I'll get down and you can get on my back. Then you can see in."

"No, I'm stronger," answered Samantha. "You get on my back."

Samantha got on her hands and knees. Nellie stepped carefully onto her back. She held tight to the windowsill and looked over. "Oh, Samantha," she whispered. "Jessie's there . . . and Lincoln, too, and . . . and . . ."

"What?"

"There's a cradle."

At just that moment Jessie looked up. She shrieked at the face she saw peering in at her. Nellie tried to duck, but she lost her balance and fell over, kicking Samantha in the ribs as she went. So it was a tangle of arms and legs and frightened faces that Lincoln found when he came outside the house. He laughed out loud.

Inside, Jessie brushed the girls' dresses.

*It was a tangle of arms and legs and frightened faces that Lincoln
found when he came outside the house.*

"I declare, Miss Samantha, I think I'll spend the rest of my life straightening you up after mischief," she chuckled. "What on earth are you doing here at such a time of night? Where's Hawkins?"

The girls looked at one another shyly. Then Samantha spoke. "We came by ourselves, Jessie. We didn't know what had happened to you, and no one would tell us."

Jessie's smile melted and she put her arms around Samantha. "My poor child," she said. "I'm sorry. I never dreamed you'd worry. But you see, I'm fine." She stood back and smiled proudly. "And now, come see my treasure." She went to the cradle and lifted out a tiny blanketed bundle. She brought it over to the girls and announced, "This is Nathaniel."

Wrapped in the blanket was the tiniest person Samantha had ever seen. His skin was the same fine brown as his mother's, and his head was covered with soft black curls. His cheeks were so round and soft that Samantha couldn't resist reaching out to touch them. When his tiny pink mouth opened and closed, she was sure he smiled at her. "Oh, Jessie," she breathed. "He's beautiful."

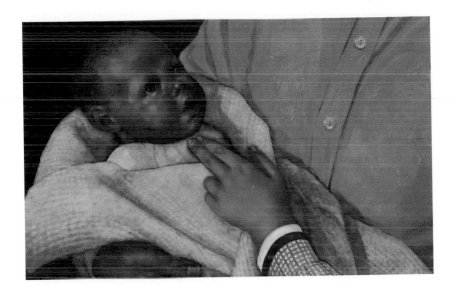

Jessie beamed and tucked the baby back in his cradle with a kiss. "But you see why I couldn't stay at your grandmother's," she said, turning back to the girls. "Lincoln's gone most of the time, working. I've got to be here to take care of Nathaniel. But don't worry, Miss Samantha. I'll come to see you often. And I'll bring Nathaniel, too." She hugged Samantha quickly. Then she hustled the girls to the door. "Now Lincoln is going to take you home. If your grandmother finds out you're gone, she'll have your hide and mine, too."

The way home seemed much shorter with

Lincoln's strong hands to guide them. Nellie and
Samantha crept into their houses without making a
sound. Samantha tiptoed quickly up the stairs and
back into her room. She hurried to unbutton her
shoes and take off her stockings. She hung her
dress in the tall wooden wardrobe, unbuttoned her
underwaist, and slipped her long ruffled nightgown
over her head. Her nightgown had never felt so soft
and warm. Her bed had never smelled so sweet or
been so welcome. She held Lydia very close and
fell asleep.

CHAPTER

SIX

A FINE
YOUNG LADY

 Two days later, Samantha tugged on the string of her tin-can telephone. She and Nellie had tied bells to both ends of the telephone, so that they could signal one another when they wanted to talk. But today Nellie didn't answer.

Samantha tugged again, but still there was no answer. She crawled through the tunnel. There was no sign of Nellie. Instead, Eddie Ryland stood there pulling gum out of his mouth in long strings and then stuffing it back in again.

"I know something you don't know," Eddie said. He looked pleased with himself, and that worried Samantha. She waited.

"Nellie is going away," Eddie said.

Samantha felt as though she'd been hit. "What are you talking about, Eddie?"

"Our driver's taking her back to the city. She's sick, and my mother says she's not strong enough to work. She's waiting in the kitchen. Mother says next time we'll get an immigrant woman who can last longer."

Samantha wanted more than anything to punch Eddie in the nose. But she knew she couldn't. She knew that even if she were a boy, she couldn't punch Eddie in the nose. Certainly a grown-up person would not punch Eddie in the nose. A grown-up person probably would not have reached out and shoved Eddie's chewing gum into his hair either. But Samantha did. After all, she was only nine, and that is only half grown-up. Then she rushed to her friend, leaving Eddie howling and trying to pull the sticky mess out of his curls.

In the Rylands' kitchen, Nellie sat on a wooden chair, swinging her legs and staring at her belongings. They were tied in a shawl at her feet.

"Nellie, are you sick?" Samantha asked.

Nellie looked up. "No, I'm not sick," she said.

"But I still cough sometimes. Mrs. Ryland is afraid I'll get sick and be a bother, so she's sending me back."

"But Nellie, will you have to go to work in the factory again? You'll get sick if you go back. And what will I do without you?"

Nellie had started to cry. "It'll be all right, Samantha. Really it will. Only I'll miss you so much."

Samantha couldn't stand to see Nellie crying. "Wait a minute, I'll be right back," she said. She dashed across the yard and into her own kitchen.

"Mrs. Hawkins!" Samantha cried breathlessly. "Mrs. Hawkins, they're sending Nellie away, and her family doesn't have enough food. We have to give them something."

Mrs. Hawkins would have been quick to help even without Samantha's begging. In a few minutes she had packed a basket with a pie and fruit, some food in tin cans, and a ham. Samantha ran back to the Rylands' kitchen carrying the basket—and something else. She put the basket at Nellie's feet. Then she placed Lydia in her arms.

"Here, Nellie. You take Lydia," Samantha said.

"Here, Nellie. You take Lydia," Samantha said.
"She'll be your friend."

"She'll be your friend." Samantha hugged Nellie
and stayed with her until the Rylands' driver came.

Later that afternoon, Uncle Gard and Cornelia
were having tea with Grandmary. Samantha was
there, too, but she was not playing and laughing
with Uncle Gard. She was sitting in her chair,
working on her sampler, because even *that* was
better than talking to grownups. Samantha was
feeling very angry with grownups. Grownups took
her friends away and never even told her why. So
she sat and stabbed the needle at her sampler, and
everyone wondered why Samantha was in such a
bad mood.

Then suddenly, even before she knew she was
going to, Samantha blurted out, "I know why Jessie
left."

Grandmary looked surprised. "You do?"

"Yes. She has a baby," Samantha said.

51

Now Grandmary was really surprised. "How do you know that?" she asked.

"Nellie and I went to her house at night, and we saw." Samantha was sure Grandmary would punish her now.

But Grandmary looked more troubled than angry. "You were very wrong to do that, Samantha," she said.

"Well, you were very wrong not to tell me," Samantha answered. She was not feeling very respectful.

Grandmary took in her breath sharply. She looked at Uncle Gard and Cornelia for help. But they said nothing.

Grandmary put her teacup down and nodded slowly. "Yes, Samantha, I think you are right. I should have told you," she said.

The room was very quiet. Samantha felt pleased and relieved. "Well, can Jessie come back?" she asked.

"Now, Samantha, you know she has to take care of the baby."

"But she could bring him with her," said Samantha. "He wouldn't bother anybody."

Grandmary looked thoughtful. "Well, I hadn't thought about that. But I suppose if Jessie wants to, and Mrs. Hawkins doesn't object . . ." As if anyone could possibly imagine Mrs. Hawkins objecting to Nathaniel!

"Oh, thank you, Grandmary!" Samantha almost shouted. But Grandmary wasn't used to making mistakes, and she was feeling embarrassed. She changed the subject. "You don't have your doll today, Samantha. Are you tired of her already?"

Samantha looked down and felt her face turn hot. "No—no, I lost her."

"You *lost* her?" Grandmary was upset. "My dear Samantha, how are you ever going to grow into a proper young lady? I try and I try to give you a sense of value and you—"

"I think Sam's sense of value is just fine, Mother," Uncle Gard interrupted quietly. "She gave the doll to Nellie. Mrs. Hawkins told me."

Grandmary stopped short. She looked at Uncle Gard, and then she looked at Samantha. Then she nodded slowly. "Yes," she said. "Yes, I think Samantha's sense of value is just fine indeed."

Samantha ran to her grandmother.

"Grandmary, we've got to help Nellie's family. They don't have enough food and they don't have enough coal. Can we help them? Please?"

Grandmary's eyebrows went up, and then she threw back her head and laughed. "Yes, Samantha, yes! I guess if you care enough to give up your finest treasure, then we can find a way to help Nellie's family." She gave Samantha a proud smile. "You really are quite a fine young lady, Samantha Parkington," she said as she opened her arms to fold Samantha in a hug as warm as summer sunshine.

LOOKING BACK

AMERICA
IN
1904

Look at the clothes, rooms, and food on these pages and peek into the stylish, "proper" world Samantha grew up in. People like Grandmary lived in large, comfortable houses. They ate their meals in elegant dining rooms. They visited with their guests in fancy parlors, where children were often not allowed at all. When children did join the adults in the parlor, proper behavior was expected. Children like Samantha would curtsy and say, "How do you do?" They would speak only when an adult spoke to them first.

STOCKINGS
No Supporters
No Wrinkles

In 1904, proper young ladies like Samantha wore dresses covered with frilly aprons, high button shoes, and long stockings held up with garters, even when they were playing. They couldn't climb trees in a pair of jeans, like you do. In fact, it really wasn't very proper for young ladies like Samantha to climb trees at all!

Imagine sitting down to this table for dinner. You would eat soup, fish, two kinds of meat, potatoes, vegetables, and several desserts. Your meal might last for three hours. It would have taken nearly all day to prepare.

The elegance and comforts of "proper" life in 1904 were possible because there were many servants

to do the work. A cook like Mrs. Hawkins spent nearly all day making meals for a family. She had to make just about every dish from scratch, since there were no refrigerators or freezers and there was very little prepared food like cake mix or canned soup.

A maid like Elsa scrubbed the floors and cleaned the sooty gas lamps that lighted a proper home. A manservant like Hawkins tended the vegetable garden in summer and the furnace in winter. He also took care of the horse and fancy carriage that people like Grandmary used instead of a car.

The lives of the servants were not very comfortable or elegant. Servants worked long days for little money. Their work was hard because they did not have many of the modern conveniences we have today. Kitchens were usually very hot because stoves

had to be kept full of glowing coals even on the hottest summer days. Without vacuum cleaners, maids had to hang heavy carpets on clotheslines and pound them with rug beaters. Servants who did the laundry didn't have washing machines or dryers. They had to iron the fancy tablecloths, frilly petticoats, and stiff linen sheets with irons they heated on hot stoves.

A servant doing laundry

Servants were expected to do this work without complaint and to keep their "proper" place—separate from the family they worked for. They ate in the kitchen after the family's meal in the dining room was over. They often lived in small rooms in the attic or above the carriage house. They were not supposed to play with the children or visit with the parents.

Even though a servant's life was a hard one, there were plenty of people willing to do these jobs. In 1904, many of the people living in American cities were poor. They would do any kind of work just to help their families survive. If they weren't servants,

59

they often worked in factories for long hours and little pay. Children like Nellie went to work to help their families earn money.

Young ladies like Samantha did not work. Drying dishes or making a bed was not considered a proper thing for them to do. In fact, Grandmary would not have expected Samantha to *ever* work, even as an adult.

But modern women like Cornelia had different ideas. They believed that women should do much more than run elegant, comfortable households. In 1904,

Women leaders of 1904

many young women went to college or studied to become teachers and nurses. They learned to use new office machines like the typewriter. They wanted to help the people who lived in city slums. They wanted to be sure that poor children went to school instead of working. They wanted women to be able to vote.

While the rules about what was proper were changing, America was changing in other ways, too. Cities were getting bigger and buildings were getting taller. Automobiles were taking the place of horses. Lightbulbs were being used instead of gas lamps. Electric irons, vacuum cleaners, and stoves were beginning to make a servant's work easier. To grow up in such a changing world was often confusing, but it was always exciting.

Women marched for equal rights.

61

A Sneak Peek at

Samantha
Learns a Lesson

Nellie's back—and she gets to go to school!
But after Nellie's first day, Samantha can't find her.

On Saturday morning Samantha was getting dressed when there was a sharp knock at her door. Elsa leaned her head in. "You have company, miss," she said. Elsa looked annoyed at having to bother with Samantha's company. "Your grandmother said to tell you it's a friend. She's in the parlor." Samantha was surprised. She had lots of friends who came to play, but Grandmary would never tell any of them to wait in the parlor. The parlor was only for grown-up visitors. Samantha hurried downstairs. She stopped in the hall to straighten her dress, then slowly opened the parlor door and looked around. At first she thought the room was empty. Then she saw a wide blue bow just peeking over the back of the green velvet chair.

"Nellie!" Samantha yelled. She ran around the chair and hugged the girl who jumped up to meet her. Nellie was laughing.

"Oh, Nellie, it's really you! You're all right!" Samantha stood back and looked at her friend. "Are you back at the Rylands'?" she asked.

"Oh, no, it's much better," Nellie said. Her eyes were sparkling. "It was your grandmother, Samantha. She did it. She talked to Mrs. Van Sicklen,

and Mrs. Van Sicklen hired my mother and father.
Dad will be her driver. He'll take care of the horses
and the garden. Mam will cook and clean and do
laundry. And Bridget and Jenny and I will help."
Nellie bounced with excitement. She looked as if she
had a grand surprise. "And guess what, Samantha?
We get to *live* there! All of us! We really do! In the
rooms over the carriage house. Isn't that wonderful?"

Samantha grabbed Nellie's hands and danced
with her around the parlor. "Oh, Nellie! You'll live
only two houses away. We can play every single
day when I get home from school."

Nellie stopped. Only her eyes danced now. She leaned over as if to tell a secret. "Samantha," she said in an excited half-whisper, "I'm going to go to school, too. Mrs. Van Sicklen told your grandmother I could." Nellie jumped a little jump and clapped her hands. "What do you think of that?"

Samantha hugged her. "Oh, Nellie, that *is* wonderful. It's just wonderful! I'm so glad you're back!" Samantha swung Nellie around in a circle and then started toward the door. "Come on," she called, "maybe Mrs. Hawkins will give us some gingerbread!"

Monday morning Samantha led a strange parade down the hill, across Main Street, and into the Mount Bedford Public School. She walked tall and proud, dressed in her best gray dress. Nellie walked next to her, skipping little excited skips now and then. Jenny and Bridget, Nellie's little sisters, followed behind. They squeezed each other's hands and walked very quietly.

Bridget was seven and Jenny was six. They would both start in the first grade. They looked shy and scared as they tiptoed into their classroom.

Then Samantha led Nellie to the second grade classroom. Nellie would start there because she knew her letters and she could read a little, even though she had never been to school before. In the dim hallway, facing the tall oak door, Nellie looked frightened. She twisted her hand in her dress and looked at Samantha for help. "Everything will be fine, you'll see," Samantha said. "Remember, I'll meet you on the front steps when school's over."

Nellie took a deep breath and stepped into her classroom. Samantha hurried out of the building and ran the two blocks to Miss Crampton's.

All day long Samantha worried about Nellie. During morning exercises she wished she had taught Nellie the Oath of Allegiance. She knew they would be saying it in the public school. Did Nellie know it? Did she know the hymns they would sing?

At lunchtime, as Samantha ate her watercress sandwich, she remembered the lard pails Nellie and her sisters had carried as lunchboxes. She wished she had looked inside. She wasn't sure they had enough to eat. At least she could have given them her cookies.

 During penmanship class, Samantha practiced S's and Q's and thought that she should have stayed longer with Nellie. Would someone help her find the pencil sharpener? Would there be someone to show her where the bathroom was?

By three o'clock Samantha was almost bursting to know how Nellie had gotten along. She ran the two blocks to the public school and climbed the front steps two at a time. Jenny and Bridget began jumping up and down the minute they saw her. Both of them talked at once.

"There are thirty desks in our room, Samantha. I can count to thirty," Bridget said.

"I have my own desk," Jenny added.

"We put our lunches in the clock room," Bridget continued.

"No, Bridget, it's not a clock room, it's a *cloak* room," said Samantha.

"We have books, see?" Jenny held up three books strapped together with a leather belt.

"That's nice, Jenny," said Samantha. "But where's Nellie? Why isn't she here?"

The little girls looked at each other and shrugged. "We don't know. We haven't seen her."

Samantha looked around. All the other boys and girls were on their way home. Samantha saw Eddie Ryland pulling Carrie Wilson's hair ribbon off and running down the street with it. But there was no sign of Nellie. Where could she be?

Then Samantha saw her. Nellie was huddled by the bushes near the foot of the steps. She was sitting on her heels with her head in her hands. And she was crying.

READ ALL OF SAMANTHA'S STORIES,
available at bookstores and *www.americangirl.com.*

MEET SAMANTHA ◆ An American Girl
Samantha becomes good friends with Nellie, a servant girl,
and together they plan a secret midnight adventure.

SAMANTHA LEARNS A LESSON ◆ A School Story
Samantha becomes Nellie's teacher, but Nellie has some
very important lessons to teach Samantha, too.

SAMANTHA'S SURPRISE ◆ A Christmas Story
Uncle Gard's friend Cornelia is ruining Samantha's
Christmas. But Christmas morning brings surprises!

HAPPY BIRTHDAY, SAMANTHA! ◆ A Springtime Story
When Eddie Ryland spoils Samantha's birthday party,
Cornelia's twin sisters know just what to do.

SAMANTHA SAVES THE DAY ◆ A Summer Story
Samantha enjoys a peaceful summer at Piney Point,
until a terrible storm strands her on Teardrop Island!

CHANGES FOR SAMANTHA ◆ A Winter Story
When Samantha finds out that her friend Nellie is living in an
orphanage, she must think of a way to help her escape.

◆

WELCOME TO SAMANTHA'S WORLD ◆ 1904
American history is lavishly illustrated
with photographs, illustrations, and
excerpts from real girls' letters and diaries.